Pass the Jam, Jim!

First published in the United Kingdom 1992
by The Bodley Head Children's Books

First published in Mini Treasures edition 1998
by Red Fox
Random House Children's Books
61-63 Uxbridge Road, London W5 5SA

Random House Australia (Pty) Ltd
20 Alfred Street, Milsons Point, Sydney,
New South Wales 2061, Australia

Random House New Zealand Limited
18 Poland Road
Glenfield,
Auckland 10, New Zealand

Random House South Africa
PO Box 2263, Rosebank 2121, South Africa

RANDOM HOUSE UK Limited Reg No. 954009

A CIP catalogue record for this book
is available from the British library.
Printed in China

ISBN 978 0 099 26344 9

Pass the Jam, Jim

Kaye Umansky &
Margaret Chamberlain

Mini Treasures

RED FOX

Hurry Mabel, lay that table!

Jane, put Wayne back in his pram!

Where's the bread, Fred?
Bread I said, Fred.

Pass the jam, Jim,
Jam, Jim, jam.

Cut the cake,
Kate.

Pour the tea,
Lee.

Who wants cheese and who wants ham?

Pass the pot, Dot.
Is it hot, Dot?

Pass the jam, Jim,
Jam, Jim, jam.

Here's the salt, Walt.
Use your spoon, June.

Jill don't spill
and Phil don't cram!

What a mess, Bess,
On your dress, Bess.

Pass the jam, Jim,
Jam, Jim, jam.

Drink your juice,
Bruce.

Slice of pie,
Guy?

Sip your soup up slowly, Sam.

Who's for custard?
Where's the mustard?

Pass the jam, Jim,
Jam, Jim, jam.

Boil the kettle, Gretel.

Bring the butter, Betty.

Charles wants chips and so does Pam.

Thanks a lot, Jim . . .
Oh! You've NOT, Jim!

JIM! YOU'VE EATEN
ALL THE JAM!